MIKE YOUNG

C000291738

SUPERTED

AND MOTHER NATURE

Illustrations by
Rob Lee and David Blake

Muller

Somewhere high above the atmosphere of the Earth floats a special cloud. It glows gently with a strange light and fills the cold emptiness of the heavens with its own magic warmth. This is the home of Mother Nature.

'Mmmm . . . I think there's a certain place on the planet Earth that deserves a little more sunshine,' muttered Mother Nature to herself, as she pottered amongst her instruments. She twiddled dials and fiddled with switches, and then sat back with a smile of satisfaction.

On planet Earth, the Sun came out from behind a cloud to shine on a tree house in the woods. SuperTed looked out of the window and frowned.

'I'm a bit worried about all this sunshine, Spotty,' he said to his friend. 'I'm going to take a look at Africa on the video monitor, to make sure it isn't becoming too dry.'

While Mother Nature busied herself with her controls, carefully adjusting the weather conditions on Earth, a large, ugly rocket was approaching. Texas Pete, Bulk and Skeleton had found her cloud.

'What do we do when we get there, Tex?' asked Bulk, as the rocket began to descend onto the landing pad.

'We'll take control of the weather,' came the reply. 'We'll have earthquakes, tidal waves, typhoons . . . heh, heh, heh! I'll turn the Earth into a wasteland.' Tex set the rocket down on the cloud with an awkward thud. Then they all crept towards Mother Nature.

A wicked grin spread across Tex's face. 'I'll force that grey-haired old goofball to mix me a potion, just like the one she gave to SuperTed!'

Mother Nature was too busy fussing over her controls to notice the three villains. They crept up quietly behind her, and Texas Pete clamped his hand over her mouth.

'Don't struggle, lady,' he snarled, 'or we'll plunge the world into chaos.'

'Yeah,' agreed Bulk, who went straight to the weather machine. 'Just like this!' He pressed a button on the control panel.

On Earth, the effect was immediate. Dalmations lost their spots and tigers lost their stripes. The zebra that SuperTed could see on the video monitor suddenly looked as if it had measles.

From outside the tree house, Spotty gave a startled cry. 'Aaaargh! SuperTed! I've got stripes!'

Meanwhile, on the cloud, Texas Pete was forcing Mother Nature to mix up the magic potion. She was not very happy and, as she poured magic ingredients from one pot to another, she turned to Tex in disgust.

'You won't get away with this, you big bully. SuperTed will be here as soon as he hears about it, mark my words.'

Tex smiled nastily. 'Shut up, you old windbag!' he said. He started to push buttons and pull levers on the weather machine. 'I'll take care of SuperTed! Just you watch!'

On Earth, the weather took a dramatic turn for the worse. Rain suddenly beat against the tree house, and the wind shook the wooden roof.

'Pulsating Prunes, Spotty!' shouted SuperTed. 'The weather's going crazy!'

'We'd better go and see Mother Nature!' said SuperTed. 'She'll know what to do.'

He said his secret, magic word, and blasted through the doorway at full power. But as soon as he got outside the wind hit him, and blew him back against a tree.

'Are you all right, SuperTed?' asked Spotty, peering down from the tree house.

'Ye..es,' said SuperTed very shakily. 'We'd better hurry!' He picked himself up, and they both began to run towards the Spotty rocket. The wind stung their ears, and the rain lashed their faces as they ran through the undergrowth. Then there was a huge flash of lightning, and a large tree started to topple towards them.

'Help!'

On the magic cloud, Tex was watching all this on a video monitor. When he saw SuperTed and Spotty disappear beneath the tree he turned away from the screen with an evil smile.

'Ha, ha, ha! That's the end of SuperTed!'

SuperTed was not that easily beaten. He struggled out through the branches of the fallen tree and helped Spotty to his feet. They set out once again towards the rocket.

Mother Nature seemed to be taking a long time to mix her potion and Texas Pete was becoming very impatient. 'Come on, lady,' he said with a vicious sneer. 'Hurry up or I'll do some permanent damage!'

Before he could carry out his threat, he was interrupted by a shout from Bulk.

'What's this, Tex?' said Bulk, looking into the monitor. 'It looks like a rocket.'

Sure enough, there was the Spotty rocket, heading towards the cloud. SuperTed was on his way!

Tex dashed to the weather controls. 'I'll soon put paid to that rocket-powered runt!' he screamed angrily, and pulled on a lever. A few seconds later, a shower of meteoroids swept towards the Spotty rocket.

'Great Moons of Spot!' shrieked Spotty. 'A meteoroid storm!' The rocket began to lurch from side to side as they tried to avoid the large chunks of rock. There was a loud crash as a huge meteoroid hit the hull, sending the rocket spinning towards the cloud.

SuperTed and Spotty watched in horror as the rocket plunged straight into the heart of the cloud.

Sparks flew and wires crackled with electricity as the rocket pushed its way through the centre of the cloud into Mother Nature's control room. SuperTed and Spotty leapt out as soon as the rocket came to a halt.

Spotty pushed Bulk straight into the controls and, whilst Mother Nature hit Skeleton over the head with her spoon, SuperTed picked up Texas Pete and hurled him across the floor. Their victory was short-lived. Texas Pete grasped a lever on the weather console and snarled evilly.

'Don't come any nearer, SuperTed, or I'll send a tidal wave to cover the Earth!'

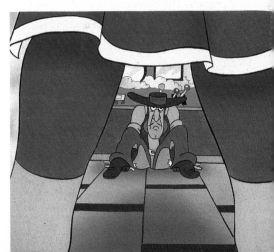

SuperTed stood back. He did not want anyone on the Earth to be hurt.

Then Tex turned towards Mother Nature. 'Come on, Grandma,' he hissed. 'Give me the potion!'

Mother Nature dipped the spoon into the mixture and took it to Texas Pete. 'I'm sorry, SuperTed,' she said. 'I haven't any choice. You know that our first duty is to protect all living creatures.' Then as Tex began to laugh with pleasure, she fed him the potion.

As soon as the mixture was inside him, a very strange thing happened. Tex began to choke and splutter, then a great sheet of flame shot from his mouth. With a loud 'pop!' he hiccupped so violently that he flew into the air.

'Oh dear,' said Mother Nature, with a twinkle in her eye. 'I seem to have mixed the wrong potion.'

Tex went on hiccupping. He hiccupped so hard that his stomach hurt and every loud hiccup sent him flying. He was no longer a danger to anyone.

Mother Nature thanked SuperTed for his help, and made sure that Spotty got his spots back. SuperTed and Spotty said goodbye and set off back to Earth, towing Tex's rocket behind them.

As they floated gently back to Earth, the silence of space was broken by the sound of loud, wild hiccups.

Books in the SuperTed series

SuperTed in Bulk's Story
SuperTed in SuperTed's Dream
SuperTed and the Lumberjacks
SuperTed and Mother Nature
SuperTed Meets Zappy and Zoppy
SuperTed and the Green Planet
SuperTed at the Bottom of the Sea
SuperTed and the Hungry Monkeys
SuperTed and the Crystal Ball
SuperTed and the Gun Smugglers
SuperTed in the Arctic
SuperTed in Spotty and the Indians